Huxley Pig's Airplane

Rodney Peppé

 **DELACORTE PRESS**

For Toby Floyer

Other books about Huxley Pig

Here Comes Huxley Pig

Huxley Pig the Clown

Published by
Delacorte Press
Bantam Doubleday Dell Publishing Group. Inc.
666 Fifth Avenue
New York, New York 10103

This work was originally published in Great Britain by Frederick Warne/
Penguin Books Ltd.

Library of Congress Cataloging – in – Publication Data will be printed in subsequent editions.

ISBN 0–385–30038–7

10 9 8 7 6 5 4 3 2 1

Printed and bound in Hong Kong by Imago Publishing Ltd.

Early one morning, Huxley Pig was wakened by the sound of the doorbell. A package had been delivered.

His granny had sent him a wonderful
present. "An airplane!" said Huxley.
"Just what I wanted!"

Huxley got dressed and played with his plane. He zoomed on his bed...

He zoomed
on his table…

Z-O-O-M

Z-O-O-M

Z-O-O-M

Z-O-O-M

and he zoomed
on his chair.

When Huxley had finished zooming, he found a letter hidden in the wrapping paper. His granny was coming to visit him.

"I'd better clean my room," thought Huxley, "or she'll think I live in a pigsty!"

"It might be easier, though," he said, "if I could go to see her in my plane."

He rolled to the left...

and he rolled to the right.

And then the engine began to cough. "Perhaps," thought Huxley, "I had better land."

It was a bumpy landing.
"Terrible pilot!" said
Horace the mechanic.

"The plane's
making funny
noises,"
said Huxley.
"No problem,"
said Horace.
"I'll fix it!"

So Horace worked on the plane
while Huxley had lunch.

"Is that it?" asked Huxley when he thought Horace had finished. "I'll go for a test flight, to make sure," said Horace. "Hop in the back."

Huxley felt
a raindrop.
Then another...
and another.
"It's going
to rain,"
he said.

"Nonsense," said Horace. "Look at the sun."

And they flew through a rainbow. "I've
never done that before," said Huxley. "Oh, I
do it all the time," said Horace.

Then it began to grow dark. "Thunder," said Huxley. "We're in for a storm." "Storm…what storm?" said Horace.

And they flew into a storm. "I can't see where we are," cried Huxley. "Please pass me the map."

"Catch,"
called Horace,
tossing
the map
over his
shoulder.

Oh rats!

"That wasn't
very clever,"
said Huxley.
"Now I can't
find my
granny's
house!"

"You'll have to find it without me!"
said Horace, buckling on his parachute.
"I don't like storms!" And he jumped.

The plane zoomed up and
Huxley nearly fell out.

He tried to scramble into the pilot's seat,
but the plane was out of control.

Wheeee! The plane plunged through the clouds into the treetops to... CRASH!

Huxley woke up with the sound still ringing
in his ears! "Have I been dreaming?"
he wondered. "But I've got Horace's wrench...
and his hat! Impossible!" thought Huxley
as he realized, "It's Granny at the door!"

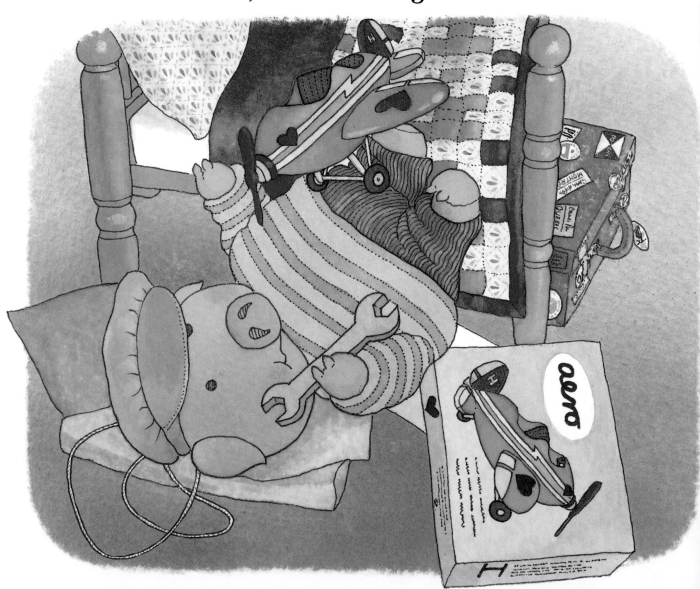